THE ADVENTURES OF

Captain Pugwash

The Portobello
Plague

D1321589

THE ADVENTURES OF
Captain Pugwash

The Portobello Plague

RED
FOX

A Red Fox Book

Published by Random House Children's Books
20 Vauxhall Bridge Road, London SW1V 2SA

A division of The Random House Group Ltd
London Melbourne Sydney Auckland
Johannesburg and agencies throughout the world

The Adventures of Captain Pugwash
Created by John Ryan
© Britt Allcroft (Development Ltd) Limited 2000
All rights worldwide Britt Allcroft (Development Ltd) Limited
CAPTAIN PUGWASH is a trademark of Britt Allcroft (Development Ltd)
Limited
THE BRITT ALLCROFT COMPANY is a trademark of
The Britt Allcroft Company plc

Text adapted by Sue Mongredien from the original TV story
Illustrations by Ian Hillyard

1 3 5 7 9 10 8 6 4 2

This book is sold subject to the condition that it shall not, by way of trade or
otherwise, be lent, resold, hired out, or otherwise circulated without the
publisher's prior consent in any form of binding or cover other than that in
which it is published and without a similar condition including this condition
being imposed on the subsequent purchaser.

Printed and bound in Denmark by
Nørhaven A/S

THE RANDOM HOUSE GROUP Limited Reg. No. 954009

www.randomhouse.co.uk

ISBN 0 09 940822 8

Chapter One

It was a grey, misty morning as the Black Pig sailed towards Portobello Harbour. Captain Pugwash and his men had just returned from another adventure and they were looking forward to being home again.

"Land ahoy!" called out Tom, the cabin boy. He was high up in the crow's nest, looking through his telescope at the shoreline ahead.

There was silence.

"I said, 'Land ahoy!' " he shouted a little louder.

Still nothing. Tom frowned. Where was everyone?

Just then, a loud snore floated up from the cabin below. "Why, they're all still asleep!" Tom said to himself in surprise, and ran down onto the main deck.

"Wake up!" he shouted. "Hey! Wake up! We're here!"

"Here," he heard the Mate murmur sleepily. Then, "Here? Food?!"

The crew were worn out from their long trip – and what's more, they were all very hungry.

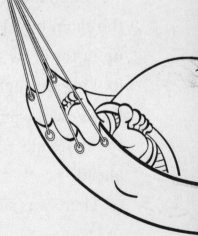

The Mate was first on deck,
wearing his stripy pyjamas. He licked
his lips. "It's been ages since we've seen
Portobello Harbour," he said happily.
"I hope the Harbour Cafe are still
serving their big breakfasts!"

Tom smiled. "I'm sure they are," he said.

"But in the meantime..." said the Mate thoughtfully, "I don't suppose there happens to be a small, stale crust of bread in the galley, is there? Or maybe just a few teeny tiny titchy little cake crumbs I could nibble on?" He rubbed his large tummy hopefully. "Perhaps even..."

Tom shook his head. "Sorry, Mr Mate," he said. "The larder is completely empty. There'll be no food until we get to shore." And off he went inside.

The Mate looked sad. No food! He couldn't bear it!

"Morning, Mr Mate," came a voice. It was Willy, struggling to do his braces up the right way.

The Mate was about to reply when...

ROARRRRR!

Willy hid behind the Mate. "Oh! Heck! Oh heck!" he whimpered. "Wh-wh-what was that?"

"Mornin'!" said Jonah, coming up the steps behind them. "Excuse me – my belly's been rumbling like a volcano all night!"

"Well, don't erupt near me!" said the Mate with a sniff. Then something caught his eye. "Ooh, look – tea!"

"Goody!" said Willy, as Tom appeared with a tea tray. "Make mine a strong one, Tom. Strong brew for a strong crew, eh?"

"Sorry, lads," said Tom, walking past them. "This is for the Captain. And it's the last tea bag we've got."

Willy, Jonah and the Mate all
watched longingly as Tom – and the
tea tray – disappeared into the
Captain's cabin.

"Roll on Portobello Harbour," said
the Mate, feelingly. "And the Harbour
Cafe!"

"Not half," said Willy. "I'm gonna

have me a nice bit of kipper, two
slices of toast..."

"Sausage, double egg, bacon..."
added Jonah, ticking them off on
his fingers.

"One of them with Marmite..."
Willy continued.

"Tomato..." put in the Mate.

"Yeah, tomato," agreed Jonah.

"Toast..."

"Marmalade..."

"Mushrooms..."

"And as many cups of tea as we can drink!" said the Mate.

Meanwhile, Captain Pugwash was enjoying his pot of tea, and munching away at the last packet of crackers on the ship.

"Delicious!" he said, wiping crumbs off his jacket. He reached into the packet for another – but all he found were more crumbs. He'd eaten the lot! "Are you sure that's the end of my emergency supplies?" he said.

"Afraid so, Captain," Tom answered, clearing away the breakfast things.

Pugwash sighed. "Ah well." Then he tapped the side of his nose. "Still, Mum's the word, eh? What's a few crackers between friends, anyway?"

Back on the main deck, the others were still talking about their favourite subject – food!

"You've got to hand it to the Captain," Willy said admiringly. "All these days without grub and he hasn't complained once. Heroic, that's what he is."

"That's the Captain for you," agreed the Mate.

Just then, the 'heroic' Captain appeared on deck. "What ho, me hearties!" he cried.

Willy and the Mate were about to reply when...

RRRROOOOAAARRRRR!

Pugwash jumped. "Clattering collywobbles! What was that?" he said.

The others all turned to look at Jonah, who was rubbing his tummy. "Sorry, Captain. Just looking forward to breakfast," he said, guiltily.

"Food!" Pugwash snorted. "Can't you think about anything else?"

Willy and the Mate exchanged looks. The Captain really was made of strong stuff!

"Ship ahoy!" called Tom suddenly, from the look-out. He peered closely through his telescope. "Uh-oh – it's the Flying Dustman, Captain! She's in port!"

Willy, Jonah and the Mate clutched at each other in fright when they saw the ship looming up through the mist.

The Flying Dustman belonged to
Cut-throat Jake – Pugwash's sworn
enemy!

"Oh heck!" wailed Willy.

"No good will come of this, mark
my words," said a quivering Jonah.

Pugwash gave another snort,
although inside he was feeling a little
bit scared, too. "Pull yourselves
together, crew! You're not afraid, are
you, Mr Mate?"

The Mate's teeth were chattering.
"N-n-n-no, Captain!" he stuttered.

Suddenly, a bell rang in the
distance. Tom grabbed the telescope
again. "Look!" he said, pointing
ahead. "What is that?"

Through the mist, the crew saw a
hunched figure squatting on a large
rock near the harbour.

As the Black Pig drew nearer, the figure stood up and waved its arms wildly in the air. "Beware!" it wailed in a deep voice.

Tom frowned. Where had he heard that voice before?

"Beware!" wailed the figure again.

"Beware the Portobello plague! Run for your lives! Go! Don't come ashore here. Oh no! Everyone's got spots and bellyache and things like that! Beware the plague! Oh, BEWARE!"

Chapter Two

Captain Pugwash looked at his crew fearfully. "P-p-p-plague? P-p-p-p-portobello p-p-p-plague?" he stammered. "Oh no! That's bad! That is BAD!"

"Is that the one where all your hair drops out and your face goes green?" asked Willy, trying not to look too terrified. "Or do you just get big black boils all over your body?"

"Does that mean we can't have breakfast?" Jonah wailed. "But I'm starving!"

"I'll see if I can catch us some fish,"

said Tom. "And while I'm doing that the Captain will come up with a plan."

"Just what I was going to say," the Captain said importantly. "You run off and catch some fish first though, Tom. I can't possibly make a plan on an empty stomach!"

Not far away, the hunched figure that had called out the warning was removing his hooded cloak... and laughing loudly! For underneath the cloak it was none other than Cut-throat Jake!

"Ha ha! I've fooled him this time!" Jake chortled, stroking his big black beard. "Did you hear me out there, lads? Was I good or was I good?"

Jake's crew sniggered. They were all sitting around on the deck of the Flying Dustman.

"You was well good, boss," said
Stinka. "You've got 'em there!"

"The goodest!" said Swine.

"Blindin', boss," agreed Dook.
"Blindin' bit of acting!"

Jake smiled his wicked smile,
showing all his chipped yellow teeth.

"So we can safely say that Captain Horatio Pugwash really believes there's a plague on shore – and it's all down to me!"

Jake and his crew laughed louder than ever. They loved getting one over on Pugwash!

But what they didn't know was that Tom was close by, and he could hear every word they were saying from his rowing boat.

Tom smiled grimly. "I might have known," he muttered to himself. "Jake is up to his tricks again, eh?"

Still, Tom knew one thing now – if there was no Portobello plague, it was quite safe for him to row ashore and stock up on a hearty breakfast for the crew. What a nice surprise that would be for them!

Cut–throat
Jake and his
men were
still laughing
loudly so
they didn't
hear Tom's oars
splashing through
the water as he rowed ashore. They
were far too pleased with themselves
to pay attention to anything else!

"So, listen," Jake was saying,
"Pugwash and his pathetic
crew are on the Black Pig
with no food."

"Not a crumb!" put in
Stinka with a chuckle.

"Not a crust!" added
Dook, a grin spreading
over his big round face.

"And believe me, boys, Pugwash without pudding is like a cannon with no cannonballs," Jake said happily. "So what does that mean?"

His crew looked at each other, puzzled.

"Er..." said Swine, scratching his head.

"Duh..." said Dook, frowning in confusion.

"It means that in no time at all Pugwash will be as weak as a kitten," Jake told them with a grin. "And then we'll storm in and seize the Black Pig! You just see if we don't!"

Chapter Three

Captain Pugwash sat in his cabin and made a sad little groaning noise. "I'm hungry," he said. "I'm starving. I'm as weak as a kitten!"

He began rummaging desperately through his chest of drawers. "I'm sure I had another emergency supply of crackers somewhere. I can't have eaten them all!" he said. "But where are they?"

The Mate looked on in surprise. The Captain had seemed so strong earlier that morning, and now he seemed to be desperate for a crumb of anything!

He cleared his throat. "The 'uman body can last many days without sustenance, Captain. If it makes you feel any better," he said encouragingly.

Pugwash glared at him. "It doesn't!" he snapped. Then he started looking through his sock drawer. "I'm sure I had a mint humbug in here. Just one!" he wailed, throwing socks everywhere.

"Oh, it won't be like this on the Flying Dustman," he said enviously. "Cut-throat Jake always has plenty of food on his ship." He stopped searching suddenly and turned to the Mate, wringing his hands. "But how do we get it?"

The Mate sighed, patting his empty belly. "That is a good question, Captain," he said heavily.

Pugwash's shoulders drooped as he pushed the sock drawer shut again. "I give up!" he said. "Come on, Mr Mate. Let's see what Tom has managed to catch for breakfast – if anything!"

Up on the deck, Willy and Jonah were sitting mending fishing nets and trying not to think about their poor empty tummies. But every now and then, Jonah just couldn't help letting out a loud hungry belly-rumble.

Willy looked cross. "I wish you wouldn't keep rumbling!" he moaned.

Jonah looked cross, too. He couldn't help it! "I wish YOU wouldn't keep grumbling!" he said.

Willy laid down his fishing net. "So, have you ever had this Portobello plague thingummy?" he asked.

"Not me," said Jonah, crossing all of his fingers quickly, "but my great uncle Zebedee – he had the plague." He shuddered and shook his big head. "Ooh, that were a bad business."

"What happened?" asked Willy.

Jonah looked solemn. "First, all his fingers fell off one by one," he said.

"No!" gasped Willy, staring at his own fingers.

"Yeah," said Jonah. "Then all his toes."

"Oh heck!" said Willy, staring down at his feet.

"Then everything else!" Jonah told him. "And that was the end of him!"

They sat in silence for a moment.

"It's a bad business, the plague, all right," said Willy.

"It is, that!" Jonah agreed.

Then suddenly Willy grinned. "Do you know what? When I was a kid, I once pretended to have the measles so I didn't have to go to Sunday school!" he said proudly.

Jonah looked impressed. "You didn't!" he laughed. "How did you pretend?"

Willy puffed his chest out. "Well, I painted red spots all over me face, didn't I?" he said.

"You didn't!" said Jonah.

"I did," said Willy, and laughed. "I was quite clever as a child, me!"

Jonah laughed, too – so loud that the pair of them didn't notice Pugwash had come up behind them and was listening to their conversation.

A smile slowly spread across Captain Pugwash's face. "Aha!" he

cried in delight. "I do believe I've just
had a fantastic idea!"

The Mate beamed. Did this mean
his captain had thought of a way to
get them a good breakfast, other than
fish for it? Oh, he hoped so!

Captain Pugwash led the crew to
his cabin, where he told them all
to sit down.

"I have thought of
a masterful way of
tricking Jake and
his shilly-shallying
shipmates!" he
chortled. "We
shall pretend
we have the
Portobello
plague!"

"I don't want my fingers falling off,
Captain," said Willy anxiously,
checking they were all still firmly
attached.

Captain Pugwash snorted. "Your
fingers are safe, Willy," he said. "It's
only a pretend!" He paused for
thought. "What we'll do, is get on
board the Flying Dustman –
pretending to have the plague – then
they'll jump ship in fright, and we'll
nab all their food!"

"Do you think they'll have
sausages?" Jonah asked dreamily,
licking his lips.

"Bound to," said Captain Pugwash
happily. "I can almost smell them
from here!"

"Pretend we've got the plague!" said
Willy. "I get it. What a brilliant idea!"

The Mate was the only one looking
unsure. "Do they definitely have lots
of food on the Flying Dustman?" he
asked. "Only I'm feeling kind of

desperate..."

"I hope they have kippers!" Jonah said, lost in thought.

"Don't worry," said Captain Pugwash. "They always have mountains of food. And they even have a cook!"

Chapter Four

On the Flying Dustman, dinner was
being served. Captain Pugwash was
right – the crew did have a cook –
Cut-throat Jake's mum! She had
worked on many ships in her
day, but now she was getting
on a bit she was not only
losing her memory for recipes,
but losing her sight as well.

Unfortunately, on this
particular day, she had
managed to lose her glasses
somewhere on the ship, so
while she was making her

famous ratapooey stew, she had to
guess at some of the ingredients. "A
pinch of this, a pinch of that," she
muttered to herself as she threw meat,
vegetables and herbs into the large
bubbling cauldron by her side.

"A dollop of bat-spit sauce," she
said, pouring some in,

but as she turned round to put the bottle back on the shelf she knocked something into the cauldron. Oh well, she thought to herself, probably nothing more than a big potato – the more ingredients the merrier! Then she stood back, pleased with herself. "Grub's up, lads!" she called. "Come and get it!"

Jake, Dook, Swine and Stinka all appeared within seconds, sniffing hungrily.

"There you go," Mrs Jake said merrily, sploshing out some of the ratapooey onto each plate. "Eat it while it's hot!"

"Yum," slurped Stinka. "Very yum."

"Mmm, lovely, Mrs Jake," said Dook with his mouth full.

Mrs Jake beamed. "My little Jakey has always loved his mum's ratapooey," she said, trying to tickle Jake under the chin. "It's his favourite, isn't it, Jakey-wakey?"

Swine spluttered into his sauce.

Stinka giggled.

Dook's shoulders shook, as he tried not to laugh.

"Mum!" Jake thundered, turning pink. "That's enough!"

Mrs Jake fixed him with a stern look. "Don't you forget, you're not too old to go over my knee, young man!" she told her son. "Now eat your dinner!"

⚓

Meanwhile, over on the Black Pig, Captain Pugwash and his crew were preparing for their plague trick. The Mate had borrowed Willy's red felt-tip pen and was busy drawing spots onto everybody's face. Willy and Jonah were practising some bloodcurdling, plague-suffering groans to add to the whole effect.

"That's good, boys!" chuckled Captain Pugwash. "Shivering starfish, that's good! Keep it up and we'll have them running for cover – while we run for their food!"

Then the four of them climbed into
a rowing boat and set off towards the
Flying Dustman – just as Tom was
rowing back to the Black Pig with a
boat full of tasty goodies. It looked
like they were going to have the biggest
breakfast ever seen!

As Captain Pugwash, the Mate,
Jonah and Willy came aboard the
Flying Dustman, Cut-throat Jake and
his men were finishing the last slurps
of the ratapooey. Pugwash led his men
as quietly as possible across the deck
and they hid behind a pile of boxes
marked 'Pirate Brew'.

Stinka burped contentedly and set
his knife and fork down on his empty
plate. "Ahhh! That's more like it!"
he said. "Nice one, Mrs J!"

"How about a tot of grog to finish
off?" suggested Jake.

"Yeah!" they all cheered, and he
filled their mugs up, one by one.

"Can't beat a bit of grog," Swine said happily, taking a swig.

Jake's mum sniffed. "Aren't you gonna give me a toast, then?" she asked.

Dook frowned. "Ooh, I'll have a bit of toast, too," he said.

Jake cuffed him. "You idiot! She means propose a toast! Like, to the chef!" He raised his mug in the air, but Dook still didn't understand.

"To the chef on toast," he said, sounding confused.

"Egg on toast, did you say?" Stinka put in.

"Toast the chef!" sniggered Swine.

Just as they all raised their mugs, four faces covered with spots popped up from behind the boxes of Pirate Brew, and Jonah and Willy groaned their most terrible groans.

"Aaargh!" yelped Stinka. "They've got the plague!"

Even Cut-throat Jake was shocked. "I don't believe it!" he cried.

"Eeek!" squealed Jake's mum, and locked herself in the powder magazine.

"We're done for!" moaned Dook. "Doomed!"

Jake frowned. "They can't have the plague!" he said, puzzled. After all, there WAS no Portobello plague – he'd made the whole thing up!

"Well I'm afraid we do," said Pugwash triumphantly. "We have lots of horrible plague germs all over us – and we're spreading them to you, right now!"

Just then...

ROOOOAAAAARRRRRRRR!

Everyone jumped. Jonah looked at
the floor guiltily.

"See!" said Pugwash. "Hear that?
That's the plague belly-gurgles, that is.
Why, he's near to death, that one!"

"Keep away!" shouted Swine.
"Unclean! Unclean!"

Jake's crew backed away in fear,
and Pugwash's men advanced
at once.

"After them!" yelled
Pugwash. "Chop, chop!
Don't shilly-shally!"

"Don't let them
near you!" warned
Jake.

"Blow on them!
Breathe on them!"
Pugwash called in
delight, thoroughly

enjoying himself now. "Blow for all you're worth, boys!"

Willy ran after Dook, Jonah ran after Stinka, and the Mate chased after Swine.

"I'll huff and I'll puff and I'll blow you all down!" Jonah shouted as he ran, rumbling louder than ever.

Pugwash went after
Jake, his old
enemy. But
just when
the Captain had nearly caught
up, Jake turned round and threw his
mug of rum all over Pugwash's face.
And as bad luck would have it, all
Pugwash's red felt-tip spots started
to run down his face!

Jake grinned his most terrible grin
as the truth became clear.

"So! Our Captain Pugwash has
spots that wash off, does he? Plague,

d'you call it?" He took a step closer
to Pugwash and laughed in his face.
"I'd say you were in a pretty pickle
now. A pretty pickle indeed!"

The others stopped in their tracks
and came to inspect the shame-faced
Captain for themselves.

"They ain't real spots!" Dook said
indignantly.

"They was trying
to trick us!" Swine
agreed, putting his hands on his hips.

"Is it safe to come out yet?" quavered Jake's mum from behind the powder magazine door.

"Don't worry, Ma!" Jake called. "We're safe – but they ain't!"

"They ain't safe at all!" Stinka said, shaking his head. "They're in deep do-do now, ain't they, boss?"

Jake smiled. "Oh my, oh my," he said softly to Captain Pugwash. "It's all gone a bit wrong for you, hasn't it?"

To his crew, he just said, "Seize 'em! And tie 'em up – tight!"

Chapter Five

Tom reached the Black Pig with a
smile on his face. The men would be
so pleased when they saw the fine
breakfast he'd put together for them.
He chuckled to himself, imagining the
Mate's face when he dished him up a
plate of sausages and bacon. And how
Willy would smile when he saw the
kippers he'd bought!

He climbed aboard and unloaded
the bags of provisions.

"Mr Mate!" he called. "Jonah!
Willy! I'm back!"

There was silence.

He looked up and
down the deck
of the ship.
Nothing.
Then he
caught
sight of
the Flying
Dustman, moored not
too far away. He grabbed the ship's
telescope and looked through it.

"Uh-oh," was all he said.

On the Flying Dustman, Cut-throat
Jake was teasing Captain Pugwash
and his men, who were now tied to the
ship's mast. "Hungry, are we?" he
asked Willy with a horrid smile.

"Oh, heck, yes," Willy said eagerly.
"I don't suppose you could..."

Jake gave him a hard stare and Willy's voice tailed away. "No, I suppose not," he muttered.

"What a shame," Jake sneered. "I'm just going to have to let you all starve

to death, I'm afraid. And then do you know what I'm going to do?" he asked Jonah.

"N-n-n-no," Jonah stammered, too scared to feel hungry any more.

"I'm going to go over to that silly little Black Pig ship over there – and have it for my own!" Jake announced. "Two-ships Jake, they'll call me!"

"Yeah!" cried Stinka.

"Good plan, boss!" agreed Dook.

"B-b-b-but..." Pugwash began – and then stopped as each member of Jake's crew suddenly keeled over on the deck, and began

groaning and clutching their bellies
in agony.

It looked like the worst cases of
stomachache ever seen in Portobello –
all their faces were bright green!
"Jittering jellyfish!" gasped Pugwash.
"The plague! They really have gone
down with the plague!"

Just then, Tom arrived. He looked
at his crew all trussed up and helpless
– and Jake's crew rolling around on the
floor like babies. What on earth had
been going on?

"Try not to breathe!" Pugwash
urged his men. Then, as Jonah's face
started going purple, he added, "Try
not to breathe any germs in, anyway!"

"What's happening?" asked Tom.

"I want my mummy!" wailed Dook.

"I'm dying!" groaned Swine.

"Ma, save me!" moaned Jake.

Jake's mum reached over to put an
arm round her son. "Don't worry,
my baby, Mummy's here. Don't cry,
Jakey-wakey!"

Tom went over to the cauldron.
"Ugh... look at this!" he cried in
disgust – and fished out a large dead

rat from the ratapooey stew.

"Don't get too near them, Tom, they've got the plague!" warned Captain Pugwash.

Tom went over and untied the Captain and his crew. "Don't worry, Captain," he said. "There is no plague in Portobello. It was just a hoax!"

"But there must be!" Captain Pugwash said. "Look at the state of them!"

"No – that's just a bad case of food poisoning," said Tom, holding up the rat by its tail. "There really was a rat in the ratapooey!"

"Rat-a-what?" asked Captain Pugwash in disbelief.

Jake's crew all groaned at the same time. "Pooey!" they said together.

Mrs Jake blinked. "Well, I never! How did a rat get in my ratapooey?" she asked in surprise.

"Come on, let's leave them to it," said Tom. "I've got a smashing breakfast waiting for you all back on the Black Pig!"

And so he had! It wasn't long
before the crew were all tucking into
eggs, toast, sausages, bacon, kippers
and steaming mugs of tea.

"Ratapooey poisoning! Serves
them right!" chuckled Captain
Pugwash, helping himself to more
sausages.

Jonah pursed his lips and said in
a high-pitched wobbly voice, "Don't
worry, Jakey-wakey, Mummy's here!"

They all roared with laughter.

Captain Pugwash looked smug.
"Just as well I had that brilliant idea
about the spots, eh, me hearties!" he
said. "Otherwise we'd never have seen
poor little Jakey-wakey get his
comeuppance!"

"It was a brilliant idea," said Willy
warmly. "I don't know how you

manage to think of 'em!"

Pugwash took another mouthful of toast and smiled around the table. "All I can say is, thank goodness we don't have a cook!"

Tom poured the Captain another cup of tea and said nothing. He was only the cabin boy, after all...

THE ADVENTURES OF
Captain Pugwash

Join Captain Pugwash on another swashbuckling adventure!

The Double-dealing Duchess

Captain Pugwash accepts a paying passenger who is not all she seems. Pugwash is blinded by money, but Tom smells a rat. Will he be able to unveil her true identity?

ISBN 0 09 940819 8
£2.99

THE ADVENTURES OF
Captain Pugwash
™

Join Captain Pugwash on another swashbuckling adventure!

The Treasure Trail

Old Jock Badger McShovel has died and left two cryptic clues in his will – one leads to his treasure, the other to a spade. But which one is the real treasure and who will win this tricky treasure trail?

ISBN 0 09 941299 3

£2.99

THE ADVENTURES OF Captain Pugwash™

Join Captain Pugwash on another swashbuckling adventure!

Digging for Diamonds

A treasure map inside Willy's screechy violin leads Pugwash and his crew to the grounds of the Governor's house. To dig up the diamonds Pugwash must outwit the guards, and watch out for that greedy Cut-throat Jake!

ISBN 0 09 941302 7

£2.99